monarch butterfly

lightning

dragon's blood tree

honeybee

bumblebee

elk

lady fern

brain coral

For my parents: strong limbs from whom I branched —J. S.

For my beloved dad —B. K.

frost

Clarion Books is an imprint of HarperCollins Publishers.

We Are Branches
Text copyright © 2023 by Joyce Sidman
Illustrations copyright © 2023 by Beth Krommes

ISBN 978-0-35-853818-9

The artist first drew black-and-white images on scratchboard
panels, then transferred the pictures onto paper, and added
watercolor to create the illustrations for this book.
Typography by Whitney Leader-Picone
23 24 25 26 27 RTLO 10 9 8 7 6 5 4 3 2 1

First Edition

We Are Branches

baobab tree

Words by
Joyce Sidman

Pictures by
Beth Krommes

CLARION BOOKS
An Imprint of HarperCollinsPublishers

Look
how we grow:
lifting toward the sun,

spreading wide
to catch each
drop of light.

red alder

Oregon white oak

madrona

Look
how we sink deep
in the soil
to drink
and grasp and steady.

groundwater

ponderosa pines

Shasta fir

Feel our soft strength
stretching
to sail the wind.

milkweed

monarch butterflies

coneflower

Smell our petals
unfurling with color—
the smell of unstoppable life.

American goldfinch

chicory

honeybees

Indian blanketflowers

Listen
to our beginnings:
a whisper of wet,

a trickle of song,

green darner dragonfly

lady fern

joining with others,

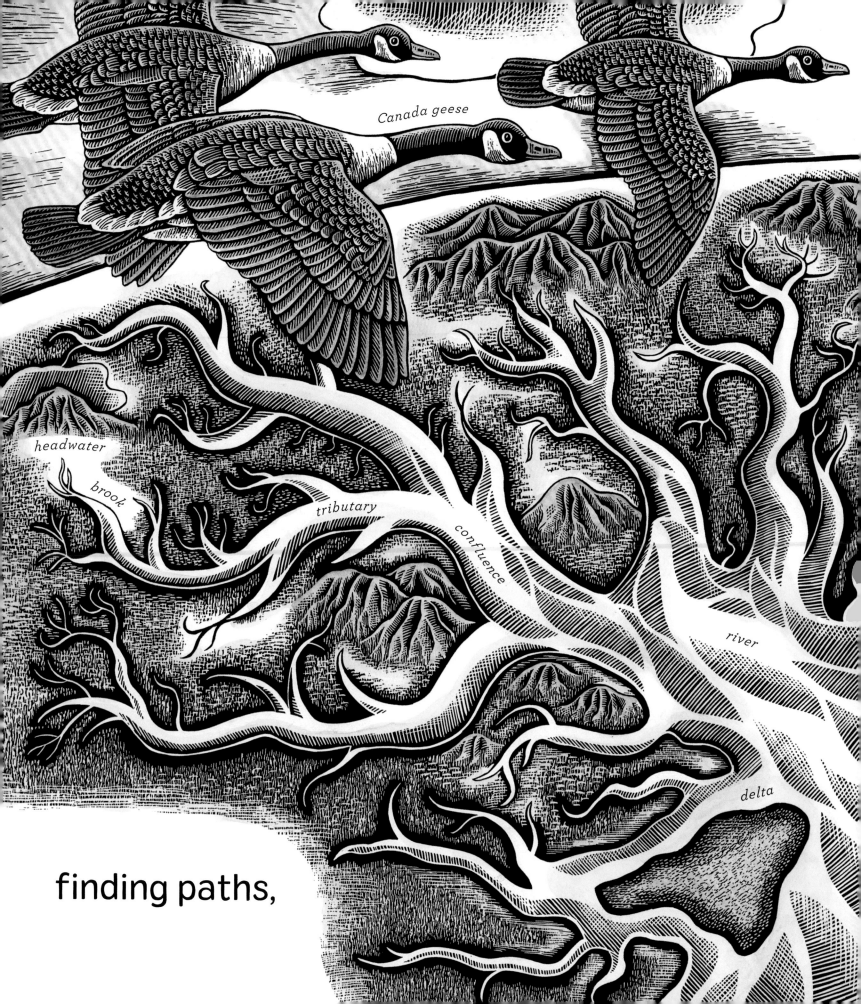

Canada geese

headwater

brook

tributary

confluence

river

delta

finding paths,

river mouth

ocean

flowing from many into one.

We crackle between clouds,
shoot downward
toward earth,

acacia tree

cloud-to-ground lightning

We splinter
rock and mud.

chuckwalla

We sprout in ice.

frost on glass

We fall softly.
Can you taste
the cool tickle
of our perfect crystals?

Roosevelt elk

snowflakes

snowy owl

From small to big,

starfish

sea plume

gorgonian corals

we repeat again and again.

dragon's blood trees

Egyptian vultures

Socotra goats

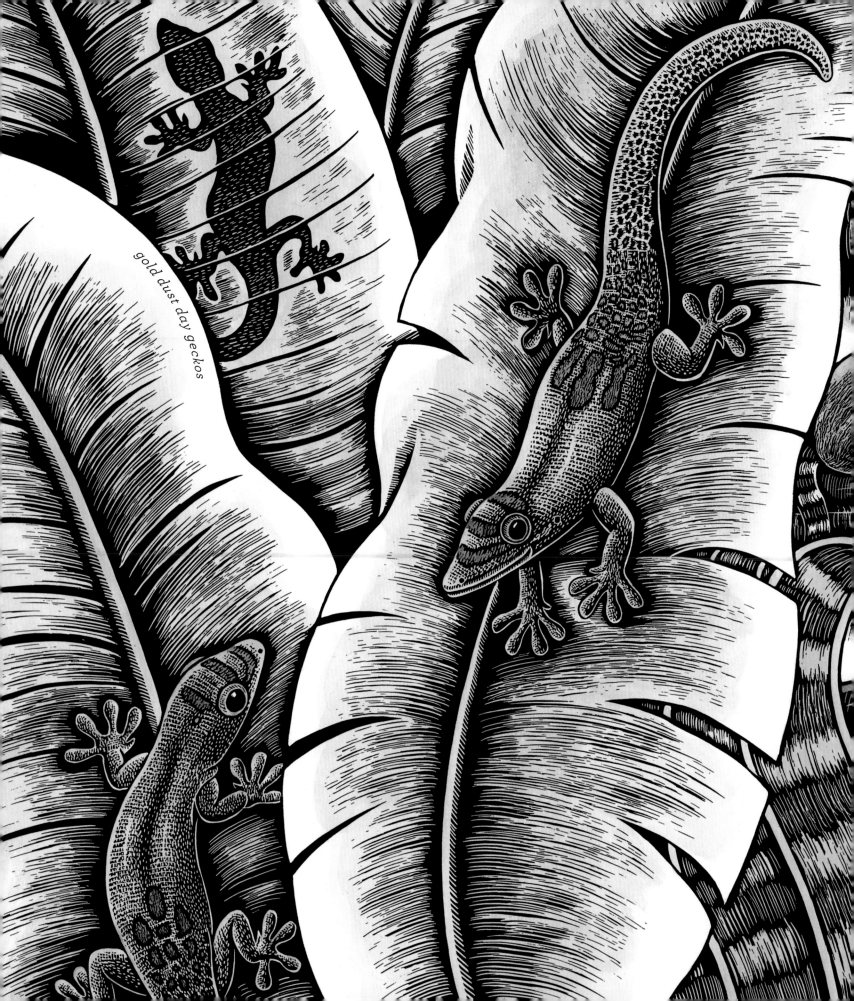

gold dust day geckos

ring-tailed lemurs

We are
strong legs that run
and toes that grip,

lesser short-nosed fruit bats

arms that stretch wide
into fabulous fingers.

We are inside you, too:
we flow and pump,
growing outward like a tree
to all your parts.

Queen Anne's lace

Then we pour back in rivers toward your heart.

goldenrod

daisy fleabane

Roosevelt elk

osprey

We are strong.
We are brave.

Oregon white oak

We are branches!

Branching: a pattern that divides into two, forming a Y

Branching is nature's most efficient way to spread something (like water or energy) from one central spot over a large area.

Branches . . . Grow

Tree limbs branch out in order to give all their leaves a chance to soak up sunlight. Leaves turn the sun's energy into nutrients, which flow back and forth through the limbs in sap-carrying channels. Tree roots are branched, too, reaching into the soil to soak up water and minerals.

Branches . . . Support

Branching provides a sturdy structure to help plants withstand thrashing wind and weather. Branching is vital to flight as well. Bird feathers hold their sleek aerodynamic form with the help of tiny branched barbs. And the delicate membranes of insect wings are supported by a network of branching veins.

Branches . . . Flow

Branches can drain large areas to a central place as well. Rivers begin as tiny trickles of water on high ground, fed by melting snow or rainfall. Pulled downhill by gravity, these trickles join others, forming outer branches of streams, which drain into a larger riverbed. As a river slows down and meets the ocean, sometimes its main channel will branch out again into a river delta.

Branches . . . Spark

Electricity also moves in branching patterns. During a storm, water droplets in storm clouds rub against each other so violently that they create an electrical imbalance (similar to static electricity). As the imbalance builds, negatively charged particles will branch out, seeking a positively charged spot—in other clouds or on the ground. When they connect: FLASH! Lightning!

Branches . . . Crack and Freeze

Have you ever seen a crack in the sidewalk? Solids like rocks, ice, and mud break along branching lines when stressed by pressure or temperature changes. Ice can also magically grow branches. Ice crystals—either as snowflakes in the air or as frost on the ground—sprout in a branching pattern as temperatures drop.

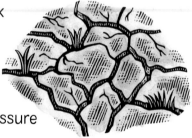

Branches . . . Repeat

One of the amazing things about branching is the way its pattern repeats at all different sizes. A huge tree branch has the same *Y* shape as a tiny twig. Trickles flowing into a stream have the same shape as two large rivers joining each other downstream. The tip of a coral branch echoes the shape of the entire coral. These kinds of repeating patterns that look similar at varying scales are called fractals.

Branches . . . Are Alive!

Your body is full of branches. It depends on them to stay alive. Powered by your pumping heart, your bloodstream branches out to every cell in your body, delivering oxygen and nutrients and removing carbon dioxide and other waste products. When you breathe, air races into your body through branched channels that lead deep into your lungs. The command center of your brain sends and receives electrical impulses through your nerves, which branch out to gather information from your senses—and to send signals telling your body what to do. Even your arms and legs are branches, allowing you to run, stretch, and grab.

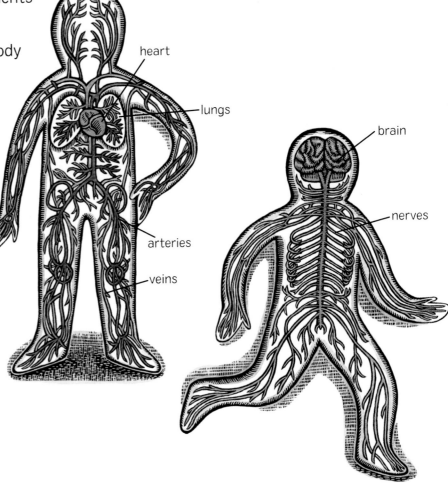

heart

lungs

brain

arteries

nerves

veins

Branches are everywhere.
Branching is the shape of life!

peacock feather

snowflake

starfish

oak leaf

elkhorn coral

gold dust day gecko

lettuce

sea fan coral

broccoli

Queen Anne's lace